GETTIN' THROUGH
THURSDAY

by MELROSE COOPER
illustrated by NNEKA BENNETT

LEE & LOW BOOKS INC. • *New York*

Text copyright © 1998 by Melrose Cooper
Illustrations copyright © 1998 by Nneka Bennett
LEE & LOW BOOKS, Inc., 95 Madison Avenue, New York, NY 10016

Printed in Hong Kong by South China Printing Co. (1988) Ltd.

Book Design by Christy Hale
Book Production by The Kids at Our House

The text is set in Horley Old Style
The illustrations are rendered in watercolor and colored pencil

10 9 8 7 6 5 4 3 2 1
First Edition

Library of Congress Cataloging-in-Publication Data
Cooper, Melrose.
Gettin' through Thursday/by Melrose Cooper; illustrated by Nneka Bennett.—1st ed.
p.   cm.
Summary: Since money is tight on Thursdays, the day before his mother's payday,
André is upset when he realizes that his report card and the promised celebration
for making the honor roll will come on a Thursday.
ISBN 1-880000-67-9
[1. Family life—Fiction. 2. Afro-Americans—Fiction. 3. Single-parent family—Fiction.]
I. Bennett, Nneka, ill. II. Title.
PZ7.C78746Ge 1998
[E]—dc21   98-13083
                                                             CIP AC

In loving memory of Fath,
who always got me through—M.C.

To my family, and all the families that
have helped me with this book—N.B.

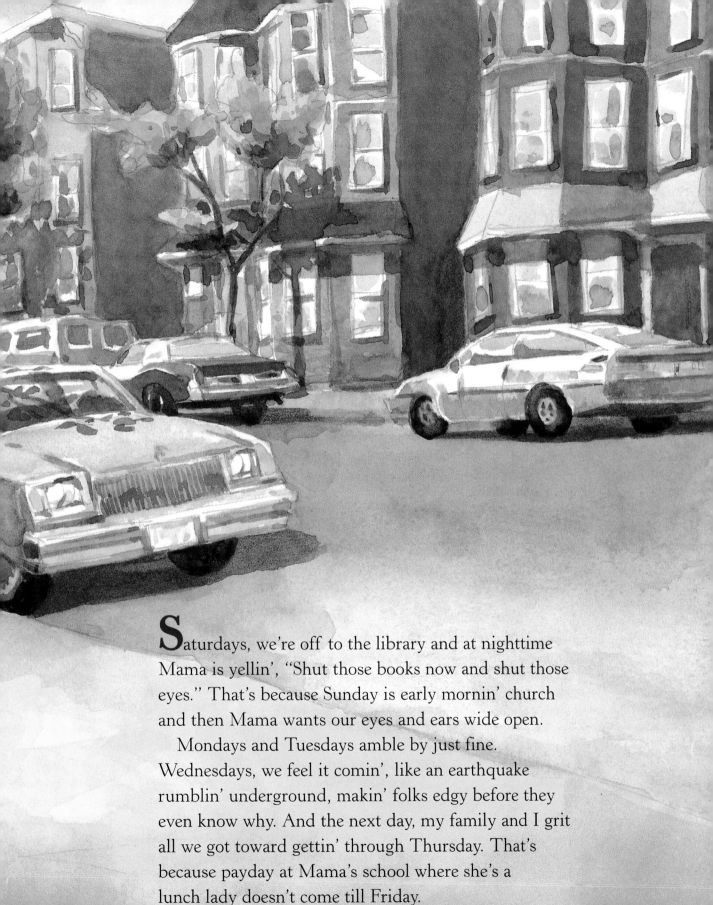

Saturdays, we're off to the library and at nighttime Mama is yellin', "Shut those books now and shut those eyes." That's because Sunday is early mornin' church and then Mama wants our eyes and ears wide open.

Mondays and Tuesdays amble by just fine. Wednesdays, we feel it comin', like an earthquake rumblin' underground, makin' folks edgy before they even know why. And the next day, my family and I grit all we got toward gettin' through Thursday. That's because payday at Mama's school where she's a lunch lady doesn't come till Friday.

"Mama, there's nothin' to drink in here." That's my
older sister Shawna callin' from behind the 'frigerator door.
"Faucet ain't broken," Mama calls back.
Shawna frowns and mumbles, but I see her put her face
to the faucet and slurp in a huge cool sip.
"Ain't no more toothpaste. Now what?" That's my big
brother Davis on the way to his girlfriend Tracy's house.
Mama swipes the bakin' soda off the shelf and hands
it to him. "Told you a hundred times you don't need
sweet-tastin' mint to make your smile sparkle."
Davis grumbles through his teeth, but when he
comes out of the bathroom, he is sparklin'.

Now it's my turn. "Chatter's hungry, Mama."
Chatter's my pint-size parakeet, throwin' an owl-size fit.
Mama opens her handbag and takes out a little plastic packet.
"Here you go, André. Lucky someone left them on a tray,
so I've been savin' them, half for today, half for tomorrow."
"Thanks, Mama." I pour some sunflower seeds into
Chatter's dish. And for the rest of the day I hear him
chirrupin' like a robin after rain.

Every week's the same. The only thing different is the things we run out of.

Every week except one.

This particular week, seemed like I had no problems. That's because of what my teacher Mr. Mitchell said the day before. Told us there were two third graders made the honor roll and looked right at me and Tricia Thomas with a big wide smile when he said it.

I couldn't wait. Report cards'd come in tomorrow's mail. Beginning of the school year Mama had said, "Any of you gets on the honor roll, we'll drop everything and throw a royal party."

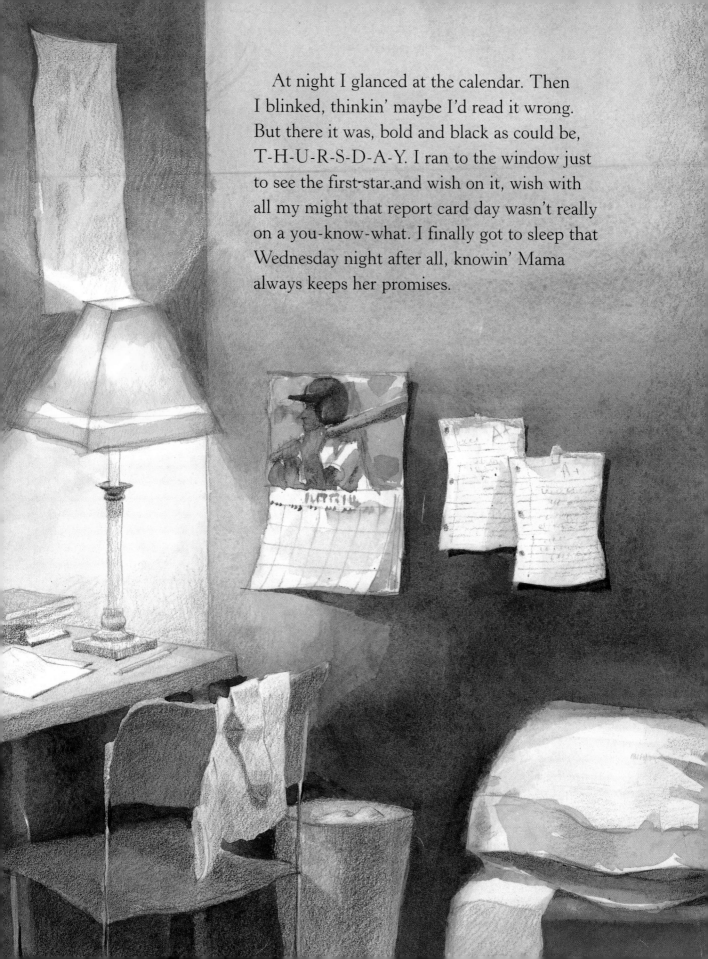

At night I glanced at the calendar. Then
I blinked, thinkin' maybe I'd read it wrong.
But there it was, bold and black as could be,
T-H-U-R-S-D-A-Y. I ran to the window just
to see the first star and wish on it, wish with
all my might that report card day wasn't really
on a you-know-what. I finally got to sleep that
Wednesday night after all, knowin' Mama
always keeps her promises.

All next day, I was jumpin' out of my skin, wonderin'
about when Mama would open her mail. I raced home from
school and there they all were, our report cards. I put mine at
the bottom of the mail stack.

Every minute crept by, slow as a wounded snake. Finally,
Mama noticed the mail. I held my breath.

She sighed at the gas bill. Made a *tsk* with her tongue
about the junk mail. Then she said, "Hmm, report cards."

She opened Davis's first. "Improvement in English, good,"
she muttered. "But what's this? Two science papers not
handed in?"

"I'll get to 'em, Mama," Davis said.

"You'll get to them *now*," she said. "But first call Shawna."

"Yes ma'am," Davis grumbled, grabbing his backpack.

"Wow," Mama said to my sister. "Eighty-nine point four
percent. Almost honor roll. You did good—really good."

Whew. For a second, I thought Shawna had beat me.

Suddenly Mama was sayin', "André, André, André!"
She scooped me into a hug-dance and whirled me
around the living room singin', "You did it! You
did it! A whoppin' ninety point three percent!"

Shawna hugged me right along with Mama. Me and Davis, we did our five-part handshake.

After a while, everybody calmed down, and Mama continued makin' spaghetti supper.

Shawna started shriekin', "My blush brush fell in the toilet. Now how am I gonna perk up my cheeks?"

"Ain't that why God made fingers, for pinchin' color into them?" Mama asked, saltin' the sauce.

"And what am I s'posed to do about my bandana? Dress rehearsal's tomorrow," Shawna went on. She was a West African woman in a play and needed a headwrap.

"Use a towel for now," Mama said, "and be thankful the real play isn't till Saturday."

Shawna stomped and slammed the door, but later I saw the zigzag towel stickin' out of her backpack.

Davis was out of loose-leaf paper. Shawna ripped a sheet from her tablet. "Here, do your math on this."

"It's s'posed to be loose-leaf," Davis said.

I looked through our junk drawer and fished out the hole puncher. Mama smiled and grabbed the paper.

Cha-ching, cha-ching, cha-ching, the puncher went. "There you go. Happy now?" she said.

Davis shook his head, lookin' at the punched-out paper. He couldn't hide his smile and soon we were all laughin' and his math did get done.

But little by little my frown took over. My problem today
was bigger than a blush brush or a turban or paper without
holes. And the night was marchin' on. I watched Mama doin'
kitchen things. She saw me eyein' her and read my mind. She
wrung out her sponge and set it aside.

"Angel babe," she said like she always did when she needed to tell me what I didn't want to hear, "tomorrow we'll have your celebration because you know what today is."

That did it. Her face got blurry 'cause my feelings were spillin' out. "I sure do know what today is! Today is report card day, not tomorrow. I don't care if it's Thursday or not. You promised, Mama. You said we'd drop everything and celebrate that very day!"

I broke away and slammed the door
like Shawna and sunk down behind it.
I heard them all whisperin' together out
there. I didn't care what they were
sayin'—I knew it was more talk about
what we can't do and can't have, all
because the day is wrong. I thought about
takin' every calendar in the whole wide
world and crossin' out the Thursdays, as
if that was gonna change things. But
sometimes that kind of daydream turns
the anger into somethin' else, and pretty
soon it's not as bad as a minute before.

"You're right, André," Mama said as she opened the door. "Report card day *is* today, even if it is a you-know-what, and we should be celebratin' like I promised. Now mind you, this is a dress rehearsal, but it's the best we can do . . . today."

Then Mama and Davis and Shawna broke into a "Happy Report Card Day to You" chorus. Shawna held a pretend plate and set it on the coffee table.

"Okay," said Davis, pretending to light some candles. "Make your wish and blow 'em out."

I frowned. "Come on," Shawna yelled. "What's a report card day cake without some candles?"

I blew out the imaginary candles and Mama dished up the imaginary cake.

"What about the ice cream?" Shawna said.

"Today's you-know-what, and you know what that means," Davis said.

"Right," I said, "but at least there's cake," and we were laughin' again like never before.

When we got calm, Davis pretended to take something off a pile. "Here you go," he said, handin' the thin-air package my way.

I pretended to tear off the wrappin' paper. "A Buffalo Bills pencil!" I shouted. "Thanks!"

Same with Mama's imaginary t-shirt and the pretend sports stickers Shawna gave me.

That night when Mama tucked me in, she settled
herself on the mattress and sang, *Hush, little darlin',*
don't say a word. Friday is a'comin', ain't you heard?
No matter how bad the Thursdays get, ain't never seen
a calendar skip one yet.

I threw my arms around her neck, then hugged her
song and her promise close.

The next night I got a real Buffalo Bills pencil in real wrappin' from Davis. Same with Mama's real t-shirt and the real sports stickers from Shawna. I blew out real candles on a real cake after makin' a real wish. And of course, there was ice cream!

And six days after, things were back to normal, but somethin' about me was different.

Our weeks are still the same. The only thing different is the things we run out of. We still feel the rumblin' on Wednesday and we still grit all we got. But gettin' through Thursday isn't so hard ever since I got my gifts that report card day, 'specially the one that didn't cost a dime.